Benson's Discovery

Written by: Olayinka Oyebode

Illustration by: Shazeb Khan

All the best
Oyebode.

Special thanks to:

Families and friends who have
made this book a reality.

Benson loves animals and he is always playing with them. Benson's room is full of animals and resembles an animal Kingdom. On his wall, are pictures of different animals such as lion, tiger, zebra, giraffe, dinosaur and a monkey.

Benson has so many animal collections; soft ones, as well as hard ones, plastic ones, wooden ones, large ones, small ones and even some made out of large card board boxes.

At times, Benson would wash the animals at the nursery during water play time. Sometimes when at home, he gets some of his plastic collections and wash them up with the bubble bath. He will tell the animals how they need to wash their bodies two times a day so they don't smell! He will also get the tooth brush and start to brush their teeth. Benson really loves and cares for animals!

At the nursery, Benson's teacher had told his mum how he would line up animals in the home corner or the construction area. He would speak to all the animals and order the animals in sizes usually from the smallest to the largest. He will tell the dinosaur to move to his left side and the monkey to stay on the right because the monkey is smaller. He lines them up in a single line either vertically or horizontally.

Mum had thought wisely to surprise Benson on a Saturday afternoon at the park. She wanted to add to Benson's animal collections by buying some sea animals. She bought a sea horse, a sea cow and a lobster. She then took her children to the park.

Mum had put all the animals she had bought under a large log to surprise his son. Benson loves animal so much.

Benson found one of the animals under a long large log at the park where mum hid them. He found the lobster. He wanted to pick it up but he was a bit scared to do so. His mum had watched him going forward and backwards trying to catch the lobster for a very long time.

Mum knew that Benson was afraid to pick up the big lobster. She asked Benson if he was scared. Benson's face and body language said it all. He was scared. Mum told Benson not to worry and cheered him on.

"You can do it Benson; you are a very brave boy!" Mum said. She then sang and clapped her hands saying; "go Benson go Benson go!" He moved closer to the lobster but was not brave enough to pick it up. "I will give you a clue," said mum. "Since you have been with the lobster, has the lobster moved?" Mum asked.

Hmmmmm! Finally, Benson got closer to the lobster and picked it up. He suddenly realized the lobster is not real after all. It's a toy lobster!

"It's not real! It's not real!" Benson shouted as he grabbed the lobster by its tail. He kept screaming "It's not real!" He ran a long distance as fast as a gazelle towards the end of the park. His face lit up; and his hair was flying as he ran in excitement. He must have been running against the wind. Benson was as fast as lightning.

Oh, poor lobster! Benson held the lobster so tight that he wasn't going to let go very soon. Not at the speed at which he was running. He was very strong. Benson ran the whole length of the field and he was not tired. He ran so hard looking for his twin brothers. He kept screaming "it's not real!"

Jayson and Johnson are his twin brothers and they are eight years old. Benson is just four years old and he can run so fast. What does mum think about Benson's reaction to the lobster that he found?

Mum thought that it was hilarious seeing Benson running to meet his brothers. Mum had seen enough surprise from Benson already. She saw how excited Benson had been. As Benson ran off to his brothers, mum then bent down to pick up the sea horse and sea cow so she could give them to Benson.

She then spotted her sons coming towards her and she changed her mind. Mum left the remaining animals under the large log of wood.

Jayson and Johnson had followed Benson back to where the lobster was discovered. You guessed rightly if you thought the twins found a sea horse and a sea cow under the log too.

In fact, Jayson and Johnson found the animals. "Can I have them please?" Benson asked.

The twins were reluctant to give the animals to their brother. Teasing Benson, "We should share equally," they said. "You found the lobster, Johnson found the sea horse, and I found the sea cow," said Jayson.

Mum walked to the children before a big argument erupts. She explained to the twins that the animals they found are for their brother. Benson was thrilled. He started dancing. He was doing "the floss." Benson then said to his mum; "you are the best mum ever."

Benson looked at the animals. He kept the lobster in his pocket. He pointed the sea horse towards his mum and he said, "I know this is a sea horse." Then he kept the sea horse away from mum. He pointed the sea cow at mum. He told mum "but I have never seen this type of animal before. I have no idea what animal this is. What animal is this mum?"

Mum explained to Benson that it is called a sea cow; and that it lives in the sea. "I do know cows live on the farm and not in the sea," Benson said. "Some cows live in the jungle too," mum replied. Benson, Jayson and Johnson looked puzzled and they said "no they don't. They live on the field or in the farm."

Mum said "elephants live in the jungle and ....." Johnson interrupted mum quickly and said, "mum but elephants are not cows." Mum smiled and praised Johnson for his thoughts. Then she answered Johnson by saying: "I know what you mean Johnson but Mummy elephants are called cows." "What?" The children were shocked. "Benson then asked so what are daddy elephants called then?" "They are called bulls," mum replied.

Mum is right. Mummy elephants and mummy whales are called cows. Daddy elephants and whales are called bulls. Baby elephants and whales are called calf but more than one baby is calves.

Can you think of some more daddy, mummy and baby animal names?

24

One day, at dinner time, everyone sat around the dining table for supper. Dad, mum, Benson, Jayson and Johnson. Benson's mum asked her sons, "What would you like to be when you grow up?" Johnson said "a teacher" and Jayson said "a doctor."

Benson thought very carefully and then said he would like to be "a lion." Mum smiled and she said "I wonder why?" Benson turned round and told his mum that he would like to be as brave as a lion when he grows up. "Wow Benson! You are so in love with animals that you want to be one." "Benson the brave lion," said mum.

Benson's dad listened to his son and wife. He found it so interesting. "That is very true Benson, lions are very brave." Dad said. They are stronger than all animals I guess" mum added.

Benson being thrilled by mum's statement; he slightly raised his voice and placed all the tips of his right-hand fingers on his head. Then he said, "they are the king of the jungle." Benson knew his sign language for king. That is why he had the tips of his fingers on his head.

Dad told Benson that "Kings are like lions because they must be strong and powerful to rule their kingdoms just like the lions rule the jungle." Then he continued, "the people who take care of animals must be brave too."

Veterinarians are brave because they treat animals that are sick. "Ve-te what?" Asked Benson. Dad broke the word down and said: "ve-te-ri-na-ri- an." Then he continued and said "Zoo Keepers are brave because they feed and care for animals.

Zoologists are also brave because they learn about animals. My Benson is brave because....." daddy paused and made a gesture to Benson as if to say he should complete the statement. Benson quickly said "I love animals. I wash my animals every day and brush their teeth."

Mum told dad about what happened at the park. She mentioned how Benson discovered an unreal lobster. "I was not brave at first but I became brave the moment I knew it was not real" Benson uttered.

"That's it Benson! You have given your mum and I an idea. We are taking you on a trip to the zoo this summer to see live animals" said dad. Whispering into Benson's ear, he said "however, your birthday is this weekend and I know what to get you." Daddy whispered what to get Benson. He was so delighted and gave his dad a big hug.

Can you guess Benson's birthday gift? It's a trip to the pet shop to buy Benson a live hamster. Dad and mum then promised to take the children to the zoo in the summer.

The End

About the Author

Olayinka is passionate about working with children particularly early years children. She has over twenty four years' experience of working with children. She graduated with BA Honours in Education and Health Studies and holds a Post Graduate Certificate in Early Years Practice. She also possesses the Early Years Professional Status (EYPS).

Olayinka is zealous about empowering and educating parents on social media on how to engage their children with different activities in their various homes and the impact of those activities on the children.

Her hobbies are singing, exercising, encouraging and developing physical literacy at every opportunity with the children. Moreover, she enjoys holding music and movement session with early years children within her community.

THE OFFICIAL NEWCASTLE UNITED
ANNUAL 2017

NEWCASTLE UNITED

Written by Mark Hannen
Designed by Uta Dohlenburg

Thanks to Michael Bolam, Stan Gate, Lee Ryder, Paul Joannou and Isobel Reid

A Grange Publication

©2016. Published by Grange Communications Ltd., Edinburgh, under licence from Newcastle United Football Club. Printed in the EU.

Photographs © Serena Taylor and Getty Images

ISBN: 978-1-911287-11-7

Welcome to the Official 2017 Newcastle United annual. After a disappointing 2015/16 campaign, everyone at the club is hoping and aiming for a successful 2016/17 season. Thank you for your continued support and enjoy the read.

Contents

BACK IN TYNE

There are some amazing old photographs which trace the history of Newcastle United over the years. There weren't that many taken back in the early 20th century, unlike the digital era we live in today, so they should be treasured for the insight they provide. Here we show you four which you may never have seen before – enjoy!

The setting is Wembley Stadium and Newcastle United and Aston Villa are about to contest the 1924 FA Cup final which the Magpies won 2-0. Here, HRH Duke of York meets the players.

It's the roaring 20s and four United stars of the era are pictured about town. (l-r) Tom McDonald, Alf Maitland, Neil Harris and Tom Curry

The United team in August 1926. That season, 1926/27, they would go on to lift the First Division Championship. Captain Hughie Gallacher is right in the middle of the picture.

This is a great picture showing the United team in London before taking part in the 1905 FA Cup Final against Aston Villa. Pictured front row in the middle is centre-forward Bill Appleyard.

A SEASON OF DISAPPOINTMENT
BUT OPTIMISM

In many ways, the 2015/16 season mirrored that of recent seasons; a struggle for most of the time with just a few outstanding highlights thrown in. However, the fact that it ended so dismally in relegation meant that, ultimately, it was a season of failure. But how many teams would sell out their stadium on the final day of the season, with their fate already sealed, and turn in their best performance of the campaign against a team that, only weeks earlier, had been potential Premier League Champions? And with manager Rafa Benitez committing himself to the club as they began the 2016/17 season in the Championship, there was plenty of renewed optimism in the air on Tyneside last summer. But for now, it's back to August 2015...

August

Ayoze Perez holds off Manchester United's Morgan Schneiderlin

Steve McClaren looked a good bet to open his season as United's new manager with a win over visitors Southampton on the first weekend of the 2015/16 Barclays Premier League season but with United heading for the three points, a late Shane Long header gave the visitors a share of the spoils. And maybe the pattern was set for the rest of the season – some good displays but an inability to gain maximum points often enough.

Papiss Cisse chests home United's opener against Southampton

The week after United lost at Swansea and that would be the first of 14 defeats on the road, undoubtedly a huge contributing factor in the eventual bottom-three finish. A draw at Old Trafford was commendable, but defeat on Tyneside to Arsenal left United up against it after only four games.

September

Three more league games but only one point gained as autumn closed in. A Dimitri Payet-inspired West Ham were comfortable winners on United's last visit to Upton Park whilst new boys Watford shocked United at Gallowgate by taking the three points back to Hertfordshire. League Champions Chelsea were the last visitors of the month and when the Magpies took a two-goal lead it looked like being a fourth successive home win over the Blues. Jose Mourinho's men rallied though and two goals in the final

Daryl Janmaat hits United's consolation against Watford

IS IN THE AIR

Ayoze Perez finds the net against Chelsea

11 minutes earned them a somewhat undeserved point. After cruising past Northampton in the League Cup the previous month, United crashed out of the competition in Round Three, losing dismally at home to Championship side Sheffield Wednesday.

October

United had the temerity to open the scoring at the Etihad Stadium, Aleksandar Mitrovic heading past Joe Hart, but hosts City responded with a six-goal blitz in an incredible 20-minute spell – Sergio Aguero ruthlessly helping himself to five of them. Two weeks later, United picked up their first win of the season, at the ninth time of asking, thumping Norwich 6-2 with four-goal Georginio Wijnaldum continuing his excellent start to the season. A nightmare derby defeat followed on Wearside, United's cause not helped by the dismissal of captain Fabricio Coloccini at a time when the Geordies were dominating the game.

It's 1-0 to United at the Etihad as Aleksandar Mitrovic heads past Joe Hart

When United drew another blank against Stoke on the last day of the month, their tally of seven points from 11 games was good enough for only 18th place in the table – and nothing would change in the next 27 games!

Gini Wijnaldum heads past John Ruddy for the second of his four goals

November

United won on the road for the first time with a televised Saturday-lunchtime win at Bournemouth. Rob Elliot, who had taken over between the posts for the injury-stricken Tim Krul, pulled off a series of outstanding saves

Ayoze Perez slots home United's winner at Bournemouth

Papiss Cisse scores at Selhurst Park but United were well beaten

as the Magpies somewhat stole the three points from the Cherries. That was as good as it got for November though as eight goals conceded in the next two games against eventual Champions Leicester (Jamie Vardy scoring for the tenth game in a row) and away at Crystal Palace, saw the Magpies slump to one off the bottom of the league with only Aston Villa below them. It sounds simple but too many goals were being conceded, despite Elliot's fine form, and not enough were being hammered into the opposing net.

December

The Magpies crammed five league games into December and it started with a bang with successive victories over two top sides, Liverpool and Tottenham. It was something of a false dawn though as the next three games only brought a solitary point and the Magpies ended the year in the bottom three. The victory at White Hart Lane was particularly noteworthy, with late goals from Aleksandar Mitrovic and

Gini Wijnaldum seals United's 2-0 win over Liverpool.

Ayoze Perez doing the trick for McClaren's side, but only drawing at home the following weekend to rock-bottom Aston Villa neatly summed up United's wholly inconsistent season. A Boxing Day loss at home to Everton, through a fortuitous gut-wrenching 93rd-minute header, was symptomatic of United's misfortune in a game they had given their all in, but lost right at the death.

An ecstatic Aleksandar Mitrovic after his equaliser against Tottenham

January

United put on a good show in their first game of 2016 but a single-goal defeat at Arsenal didn't help them climb out of the relegation zone. Three days after yet another Third Round FA Cup exit – this time at Watford – United hosted Manchester United on Tyneside in a game they could ill afford to lose. That they didn't was due to a thunderbolt strike from Paul Dummett minutes from full-time that earned the Magpies a point in an enthralling 3-3 draw.

Aleksandar Mitrovic has just made it 2-2 against Manchester United

An in-form West Ham were dispatched with relative ease the following weekend but United reverted to type in their next game, losing meekly to a Watford side who were to beat Steve McClaren's outfit three times over the course of the season, a series of results you could say defined United's season.

Gini Wijnaldum makes it 2-0 to Newcastle against West Ham

February

Jonjo Shelvey, Andros Townsend, Seydou Doumbia and Henri Saivet had been added to United's squad by the close of the January transfer window and it was hoped these signings would give United the boost they needed to claw their way out of the bottom three. And this they did with a 1-0 home victory over West Brom, but a mauling at Stamford Bridge, where United were three-down after only 17 minutes, consigned the Geordies back to third bottom once more – relegation nerves were really starting to jangle on Tyneside. After the game at Chelsea, United had a 17-day hiatus in their schedule due to being out of the FA Cup and missing a round of fixtures due to Manchester City's participation in the League Cup Final at the end of the month.

It's only a consolation for Andros Townsend at Stamford Bridge

Aleksandar Mitrovic slides home the winner against West Brom

Rafa Benitez with Claudio Ranieri before his first game at Leicester

March

The first game of the month at home to Bournemouth was seen as pivotal to United's hopes of beating the drop but they were totally outplayed by Eddie Howe's visitors and the writing was on the wall for the under-pressure Steve McClaren. The United board decided a change of management was needed and the Head Coach left St. James' Park after less than a season in charge. United stunned the football world by appointing Rafa Benitez, formerly of Liverpool and Real Madrid, as their new manager but he only had 10 games to save United from the drop – a daunting task. Defeat at champions-elect Leicester in his first game wasn't a disgrace before a point was secured in the Tyne-Wear derby at a passionate Gallowgate.

Aleksandar Mitrovic heads the equaliser in the Tyne-Wear derby

United's record on the road was truly dreadful and even Benitez's influence failed to stop the rot at Norwich and Southampton as United began the month with successive defeats, cruelly the loss at Carrow Road coming deep into injury-time. Karl Darlow had taken over between the sticks with Player of the Year Rob Elliot having suffered a cruciate knee injury whilst on international duty. It was win or bust against Swansea next up and United did the business with a convincing 3-0 victory. Two good points against Manchester City and Liverpool followed before United ended the month with a vital three points against Crystal Palace thanks to a stunning free-kick from Andros Townsend. United were putting together a nice little run but, crucially, so were the other clubs around the bottom three which meant, sadly, United's fate was never quite in their own hands as they approached the final two games of the campaign.

Moussa Sissoko strikes against the Swans

Jack Colback levels things up at Anfield

May

Saturday 7th May was one of the defining days of the season. At 3.45pm United were level with Aston Villa at Villa Park, just needing a goal which would hopefully lift them clear of Sunderland and Norwich. At the same time, Sunderland were losing at home to Chelsea. Disappointingly, United couldn't create enough chances to win their game whilst a Jermain Defoe-inspired Sunderland scored twice in the second half to give the Black Cats all three points and when they followed that up with a win over Everton four days later, United's fate (and that of Norwich) was finally sealed.

Stalemate at Villa Park as Paul Dummett shackles Jordan Ayew

Aleksandar Mitrovic powers a header past Hugo Lloris

Tottenham were the visitors to Tyneside of the final day of the season and in an incredible finale, where the support to the team and manager Rafa Benitez was phenomenal, United at least signed off from the Premier League, temporarily we all hope, in fine style, thumping the Londoners 5-1.

PLAYERS OF THE YEAR
1975/76 – 2015/16

In this feature we look back over the last 40 years of the Newcastle United Player of the Year award. It's an accolade that is much treasured by the recipient and recorded in the history books for posterity. Sometimes the winner is an obvious one, for example Andy Cole with his 41 goals in season 1993/94, but on other occasions it's an unsung hero of the team, for example Darren Peacock in season 1995/96, when the side was packed with star names but Darren just got on with his no-nonsense defending role in the team.

1975/76
Alan Gowling
"Supermac" was the star name but Gowling outscored him 31 to 24 in the season United reached the League Cup Final at Wembley.

1976/77
Micky Burns
With 17 goals the tricky, versatile striker, and crowd favourite, did more than most to help the Magpies to a fifth-place finish.

1977/78
Irving Nattrass
Versatile defender, cultured and classy on the ball, Irving was very unfortunate not to win an England cap.

1978/79   Peter Withe
Brought for a club record fee, the tall powerful centre-forward struck up an excellent partnership with the diminutive Alan Shoulder.

1979/80
Alan Shoulder
After joining United from Blyth Spartans, the former pitman from Horden captured the hearts of the United fans with his fighting spirit.

1980/81   Kevin Carr
Local lad Kevin, solid and reliable, spent ten seasons on Tyneside and in 1982 kept six clean sheets in a row, a club record.

1981/82
Mick Martin
Nicknamed 'Zico' for some dynamic displays, Mick was a first-rate midfield player who captained the club with distinction.

1982/83
Kevin Keegan
Keegan's arrival on Tyneside stunned the football world and although United didn't get promoted, KK was in sparkling form throughout the campaign.

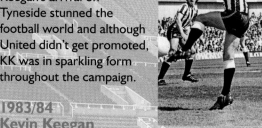

1983/84
Kevin Keegan
In his second season at Gallowgate Kevin, with 28 goals, led from the front and inspired United to promotion to the top flight.

1984/85
Peter Beardsley
Peter Beardsley and Chris Waddle shared the goals but it was the Longbenton lad who excelled in his debut season in the First Division.

1985/86
Peter Beardsley
Pedro and KK were monopolising the awards. With 19 goals and plenty of assists, Peter also played his way into the 1986 England World Cup team.

1986/87 Paul Goddard
Nicknamed 'Sarge' because of his Boy's Brigade background, Paul scored in seven successive games to save United from the drop.

1987/88 Paul Gascoigne
Gazza was exceptionally talented and was a genuine crowd-pleaser. Powerful, with amazing ball skills and great vision.

1988/89 John Hendrie
In a poor season for United, Scotsman Hendrie was one of United's few successes with many committed and exciting displays.

1989/90 Mick Quinn
Four goals on his debut against Leeds made the "Mighty Quinn" an instant hero in the famous Number 9 shirt on Tyneside.

1990/91 John Burridge
Eccentric but a top professional, Budgie played for 29 clubs in a near 30-year career – two of which were enjoyed by United supporters.

1991/92 Gavin Peacock
Hugely talented and possessing a great football brain, Gavin made more for appearances (51) and scored more goals (21) than anyone else in the squad.

1992/93 Lee Clark
In United's Championship-winning season, 'Gnasher' was ever-present and the outstanding performer in United's midfield.

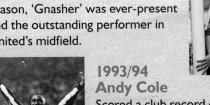

1993/94 Andy Cole
Scored a club record 41 goals in United's first season back in the Premier League, a remarkable and clinical goal-machine.

1994/95 Barry Venison
Totally whole-hearted and committed player who never gave less than 100%. Marshalled United's defence superbly from the right-back spot.

1995/96 Darren Peacock
A commanding stopper. A defender in the true sense of the word, gritty and determined but could use the ball well too.

1996/97 Steve Watson
Fantastic utility player who gave his all for the United cause wherever he played. Newcastle's youngest player too, at 16 years and 223 days.

1997/98 David Batty
Combative, energetic England midfielder who covered every blade of grass for United. A vital cog in the Entertainers' side.

1998/99 Alan Shearer
Twenty one goals in his third season on Tyneside, "Big Al" took United to Wembley only to fall at the final hurdle.

1999/00 Alan Shearer
Five goals against Sheffield Wednesday in Bobby Robson's first home game marked his renaissance – going on to finish the season with 30.

2000/01 Shay Given
United's undisputed number one who would be a vital part of Bobby Robson's teams that held their own at the top end of the Premier League.

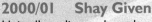

2001/02 Nobby Solano
The first Peruvian to play in the Premier League, Nobby was a gifted and highly skilled technical and creative player.

2009/10
Jose Enrique
The Spanish left-back took a couple of seasons to adapt to English football but he proved himself to be a top player, forceful and dependent.

2002/03   Alan Shearer
The Geordie legend excelled with six Champions League goals including a brace as United drew 2-2 against Inter Milan in the San Siro.

2010/11
Fabricio Coloccini
United's leading performer in their first season back in the top flight. Read the game superbly and used his vast experience to marshal the back four.

2003/04
Olivier Bernard
The French left back impressed defensively and down the flanks and his happy-go-lucky attitude endeared him to the United fans.

2011/12   Tim Krul
An ever-present as United finished fifth in the division. Tim made a number of world-class saves to earn vital points for United.

2004/05   Shay Given
Another terrific season for Shay, a commanding influence in the last line of defence and a brilliant shot-stopper too.

2012/13
Davide Santon
The Italian was a popular member of the team who could play in either of the full-back slots. Lightning quick and technically good on the ball.

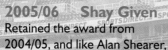

2005/06   Shay Given
Retained the award from 2004/05, and like Alan Shearer, a third time winner – a worthy award for the outstanding Irish custodian.

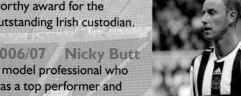

2013/14
Mike Williamson
Unassuming central defender who just got on with his job with no fuss. "Willo" impressed in the Championship and stepped up seamlessly to the Premier League.

2006/07   Nicky Butt
A model professional who was a top performer and leader in the middle of the park. Tenacious and rarely gave the ball away.

2014/15
Daryl Janmaat
Fresh from the 2014 World Cup, the Dutch right-back was a breath of fresh air on Tyneside, solid defending accompanied by dangerous forays down the right flank.

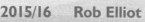

2007/08   Habib Beye
The Senegal international impressed at right-back from the off. Athletic, classy and a player who brought attacking options to United from the back.

2015/16   Rob Elliot
Took over from the injured Tim Krul and produced a succession of outstanding displays which helped propel him in to the Republic of Ireland team.

2008/09
Sebastian Bassong
Thoughtful on the ball, quick and strong, his debut season on Tyneside was hugely impressive despite the team ultimately suffering relegation.

NB. From 1990 onwards, the award was chosen by the club's programme and magazine publication team, prior to then it was a mix of supporters clubs and journalists.

GOING FOR GOAL

We have three of Newcastle United's legendary Number 9s lined up here trying to score – but only one of them can do so. Is it "Wor Jackie", "Supermac", or "Big Al"?

Answer on p.62

NEWCASTLE UNITED
INTERNATIONAL PLAYERS

Over 160 players have represented their national team whilst being on the books of Newcastle United. The majority, as you would expect, have represented England (Andros Townsend being the last one in May 2016) and we detail here the Top Ten 'Home Nations' Players (including the Republic of Ireland) with the most appearances for their countries and finish with a list of those Non-British Players who have worn their national shirt whilst at St. James' Park, together with a list of the All-Time Capped Players, regardless of their country, whilst being a Newcastle United player.

England Top 10 Appearances

	At NUFC	Other Clubs	Total Apps
Alan Shearer	35	28	63
Kieron Dyer	32	0	32
Peter Beardsley	25	34	59
Rob Lee	21	0	21
David Batty	20	22	42
Michael Owen	18	71	89
Malcolm Macdonald	14	0	14
Jermaine Jenas	13	8	21
Jackie Milburn	13	0	13
John Rutherford	11	0	11

Scotland Top 10 Appearances

	At NUFC	Other Clubs	Total Apps
Bobby Moncur	16	0	16
Hughie Gallacher	13	7	20
Kevin Gallacher	9	44	53
Andy Aitken	8	6	14
Frank Brennan	7	0	7
Wilf Low	5	0	5
Gary Caldwell	4	51	55
Steve Caldwell	4	12	12
James Hay	4	7	11
Sandy Higgins	4	0	4

1 **Rob Lee**

2 **Kieron Dyer**

3 **Kevin Gallacher**

4 **Gary Speed**

5 **Craig Bellamy**

6 **Damien Duff**

7 **Aaron Hughes**

8 **Shay Given**

Wales Top 10 Appearances

	At NUFC	Other Clubs	Total Apps
Gary Speed	36	44	80
Craig Bellamy	21	57	78
Ivor Allchurch	14	54	68
Billy Foulkes	11	0	11
Dave Hollins	11	0	11
Wyn Davies	11	23	34
Ollie Burton	7	2	9
Reg Davies	6	0	6
Alan Neilson	4	1	5
Paul Dummett	2	0	2

Northern Ireland Top 10 Appearances

	At NUFC	Other Clubs	Total Apps
Aaron Hughes	43	0	101
Alf McMichael	40	0	40
David Craig	25	0	25
Dick Keith	23	0	23
Keith Gillespie	21	26	47
Tommy Cassidy	20	4	24
Tommy Wright	16	15	31
Shane Ferguson	15	7	22
David McCreery	12	55	67
Michael O'Neill	10	21	31

Republic of Ireland Top 10 Appearances

	At NUFC	Other Clubs	Total Apps
Shay Given	82	54	134
Mick Martin	22	30	52
Andy O'Brien	21	5	26
Damien Duff	16	84	100
Stephen Carr	14	30	44
John Anderson	11	5	16
Rob Elliot	4	0	4
David Kelly	4	22	26
Alan O'Brien	4	0	4
Kevin Sheedy	4	41	45

6

7

8

Players from outside the British Isles who have won full international caps whilst playing for Newcastle United. The date listed is when they won their first cap at the club.

1950 George Robledo — Chile

1969 Ben Arentoft — Denmark

1989 Bjorn Kristensen — Denmark

1993 Niki Papavasiliou — Cyprus

1994 Philippe Albert — Belgium
Marc Hottiger — Switzerland
Pavel Srnicek — Czech Republic

1996 Faustino Asprilla — Columbia

1997 Temuri Ketsbaia — Georgia
Jon-Dahl Tomasson — Denmark

1998
Andreas Andersson — Sweden
Nikos Dabizas — Greece
Dietmar Hamann — Germany
Nolberto Solano — Peru

1999 George Georgiadis — Greece
Silvio Maric — Croatia

2000 Diego Gavilan — Paraguay

2001 Clarence Acuna — Chile
Laurent Robert — France

2002 Lomana LuaLua — DR Congo
Hugo Viana — Portugal

2005 Jean-Alain Boumsong — France
Emre Belozoglu — Turkey
Amdy Faye — Senegal
Craig Moore — Australia

2006
◀ Obafemi Martins   Nigeria

2007
David Rozehnal   Czech Republic

2008 Habib Beye   Senegal
      Fabricio Coloccini   Argentina
      Abdoulaye Faye   Senegal
      Geremi Njitap   Cameroon
      Jonas Gutierrez   Argentina

2010 Tamas Kadar   Hungary
      Peter Lovenkrands   Denmark

2011
      Yohan Cabaye   France
      Tim Krul   Netherlands

2012 Shola Ameobi   Nigeria
      Demba Ba   Senegal
      Hatem Ben Arfa   France
      Papiss Cisse
      Senegal
      Davide Santon   Italy
      Haris Vuckic   Slovenia

2013 Mathieu Debuchy France
      Moussa Sissoko   France

2014 Remy Cabella   France
      Curtis Good   Australia
      Daryl Janmaat   Netherlands
      Mapou Yanga-Mbiwa   France

2015 Mehdi Abeid   Algeria
      Georginio Wijnaldum   Netherlands
      Chancel Mbemba   DR Congo
      Aleksandar Mitrovic   Serbia

Most Capped Players of All time (whilst at Newcastle United)

1	Shay Given	Rep Ireland	1997-2009	82
2	Aaron Hughes	N Ireland	1998-2005	43
3	Nikos Dabizas	Greece	1998-2003	42
4	Alf McMichael	N Ireland	1950-1960	40
5	Moussa Sissoko	France	2013-2016	38
6	Gary Speed	Wales	1998-2004	36
7	Alan Shearer	England	1997-2000	35
8	Cheick Tiote	Ivory Coast	2010-2016	33
9	Kieron Dyer	England	1999-2007	32
10	Nobby Solano	Peru	1998-2007	29

United's World Cup Final Representatives:

Players who appeared in the World Cup Finals
whilst at St. James' Park.

1950 George Robledo (Chile)
1950 Jackie Milburn (England)
1954 Ivor Broadis (England)
1958 Tommy Casey (Northern Ireland)
1958 Dick Keith (Northern Ireland)
1958 Alf McMichael (Northern Ireland)
1986 Peter Beardsley (England)
1986 David McCreery (Northern Ireland)
1986 Ian Stewart (Northern Ireland)
1990 Roy Aitken (Scotland)
1998 Alan Shearer (England)

1998 David Batty (England)
1998 Rob Lee (England)
1998 Stephane Guivarc'h (France)
2002 Kieron Dyer (England)
2002 Shay Given (Republic of Ireland)
2006 Michael Owen (England)
2006 Craig Moore (Australia)
2010 Jonas Gutierrez (Argentina)
2014 Mathieu Debuchy (France)
2014 Moussa Sissoko (France)
2014 Cheick Tiote (Ivory Coast)

What do you remember about the 2015/16 season?

1. Who scored United's first goal of the season?

2. Who knocked United out of the FA Cup?

3. Who was Steve McClaren's first-team coach?

4. Against whom did United record their first win of the season?

5. Which team gifted United with their only own-goal of the season?

6. How many players did United use in the League, 21, 26 or 31?

7. Who left United in January 2016 for Wolves?

8. Which team did United score the most goals against last season?

9. Who made his Premier League debut on the final day of the season?

10. Who were United's two Monday night Sky games against?

Answers on page 62

Quizzes

See how much you know about Newcastle United in years gone by!

1. Which Scottish team did United beat in the semi-final of the Fairs Cup in 1969?

2. Who were the first team United beat in the Premier League in August 1993?

3. David Batty, Jonathan Woodgate and Mark Viduka all have connections with which other team?

4. Who scored United's last goal at Wembley Stadium?

5. United kicked off their last Championship season in 2009 with a draw against whom?

6. Which United goalkeeper holds the United playing appearance record?

7. Which is the only team United have played in the Football League Play-Offs?

8. United hold the record for the biggest-ever FA Cup semi-final victory, against whom?

9. Who were United's only European opponents from Bulgaria?

10. Who is the only Georgian to play for United in the Premier League?

FA CUP & LEAGUE CUP *Reviews*

FA Cup Round-Up
Rd 3: Watford 1-0 Newcastle

The FA Cup is a competition which is famous around the world and when the final comes around in May, it is one of the most celebrated days in English football. Newcastle last won the cup in 1955 against Manchester City and have been beaten in three finals since then; 1974 against Liverpool, 1998 against Arsenal, and 1999 against Manchester United.

Newcastle drew fellow Premier League side Watford in the third round at Vicarage Road. Unfortunately for United it was the eighth time in the last ten seasons that they had been drawn away in the Third Round, a bit unlucky with the FA Cup numbered balls to say the least! United had gone out in the third round for the past three seasons – four in a row was getting a bit tough to stomach.

The Hornets were Premier League new boys and up until January they had enjoyed a terrific first season back in the top flight, which had included a win against United at St. James' Park back in September. Watford made quite a few changes to their starting line-up whilst United put out a pretty much full-strength side – sadly though their demise was self-inflicted. When Gini Wijnaldum challenged successfully for a loose ball on the edge of his own box, he proceeded to inexplicably side-foot the ball directly to Troy Deeney who strode into the box and evaded Rob Elliot before slotting home for the only goal of the game.

So another season of disappointment in the FA Cup, seven third round exits in the last ten seasons and no fifth round appearance since the 2005/06 season is a pretty woeful record. Hopefully 2016/17 will bring much needed cup joy to Tyneside.

League Cup Round-Up
Rd 2: Newcastle 4-1 Northampton Town
Rd 3: Newcastle 0-1 Sheffield Wednesday

Newcastle United do not have fond memories of the League Cup having only managed to reach the final on one occasion in its 55 year history, losing to Manchester City in 1976.

The Magpies started the competition in Round Two when Northampton Town made the journey to Gallowgate. The Cobblers looked a decent outfit as they would prove as the season unfolded by winning the League Two Championship in fine style. However, on a warm Wednesday evening in August on Tyneside, they came unstuck as United comfortably ran out 4-1 winners, with goals from Florian Thauvin, Siem de Jong, Daryl Janmaat and Mike Williamson.

The luck of the draw favoured United again, as Championship side Sheffield Wednesday were next up at St. James' Park in Round Three. A lethargic performance by Steve McClaren's side was extremely disappointing for an excellent crowd of 33,986 to witness and when Lewis McGugan scored for the visitors 15 minutes from time, it was sadly no more than they deserved. United had the chance to earn a place in Round Four but they let themselves down and disappointingly bowed out of the competition with a bit of a whimper.

Can you spot the ball in this match last season between Newcastle and West Bromwich Albion?

Can you spot the ball in this match last season between Newcastle and Stoke City?

Answers on page 62

THE PROMOTION YEARS

On six occasions in their history, Newcastle United have won promotion from the second tier of English football back to the top flight, and that will hopefully be seven times come May 2017. In this feature we look back at each of those six seasons.

1897/98
Manager: Director's Committee

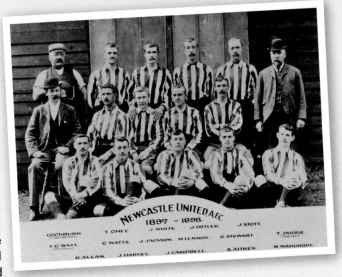

United had only entered the Football League in 1893 and for the first time, in this eventful season, United were watched by gates that averaged over 10,000. United were soon in contention at the top-end of the table, along with Burnley, and thanks to the goals from famous names of the past, Jock Peddie and Willie Wardrope, the Magpies finished the season in runners-up spot, due mainly to winning 14 of their 15 home games. Back then though, promotion was not achieved by league position alone as a series of Test Matches were played between the top sides in Division Two and the bottom sides in Division One. United came third in the mini table but because the drawn game between Stoke and Burnley was seen to be contrived by the Football League, the whole system was ditched and United were promoted in any case as the Football League decided to expand the number of teams in the First Division, and for United that was fantastic news.

1947/48
Manager: George Martin

The influential Stan Seymour had appointed George Martin as the club's new manager and his one priority was to get the Magpies back into Division One. United had a formidable home record during the season, winning 18 of their 21 games, and they would have cruised to promotion had their away form been anything like their home displays. Away from Gallowgate, United only won six games but they ground out enough points to finish runners-up to Birmingham City, finishing the season with an unbeaten run of ten games. Incredibly, United were watched by an

average home crowd of 56,300 which was an English record they held for 20 years, and for a second division side that was remarkable. Players like Joe Harvey, Frank Brennan and Jackie Milburn came to the fore and soon they would be joined by more household names, like George Robledo and Bobby Mitchell, who would be key players in the cup success that was just around the corner.

1964/65
Manager: Joe Harvey

With Wearside rivals Sunderland being promoted the previous season (United were eighth), the pressure was on the Magpies to do the same as 1964/65 commenced. And it was a former Sunderland captain, Stan Anderson, along with the likes of Jim Iley and John McGrath, who proved to be the mainstay of the side and pivotal to the club's success. A seven-game winning run from November through to January provided much optimism on Tyneside as the Magpies rose to top spot in the division. Northampton, who were surprisingly promoted with United, were thrashed 5-0 at Gallowgate and when the crucial Easter programme came around, United secured promotion in front of 60,000 joyous fans when Bolton were beaten 2-0 at St. James' Park. A point against Manchester City in the final game of the season was enough to see United win the Championship title. It had taken Joe Harvey four years to get United up, but further success was just around the corner.

1983/84
Manager: Arthur Cox

After six seasons in the wilderness, manager Arthur Cox had used the 1982/83 season to gel his team together to make a concerted push for promotion this time around. Kevin Keegan had joined the club in August 1982; Chris Waddle was a developing talent; Terry McDermott an experienced England international and, when new signing Peter Beardsley was added to the mix, then nothing could go wrong – and it didn't! United finished third behind Chelsea and Sheffield Wednesday, ten points ahead of the fourth-placed club, but it was before the days of the play-offs and United earned the third automatic promotion spot. United's front three were devastatingly effective and in a season of outstanding entertainment there were some truly stand-out performances, namely the 5-0 drubbing of Manchester City on Tyneside where the Gallowgate gates were locked over an hour before kick-off, such was the desire to see United at their rip-roaring best.

1992/93
Manager: Kevin Keegan

United had just escaped relegation to the third tier of English football the previous season so to turn things around so dramatically was some feat. With the introduction of the glitzy Premier League in August 1992, the prize for promotion back to the big time was a huge one, as Burnley, Middlesbrough and Hull found much to their delight at the end of last season. Amazingly, United won their first 11 games of the season, including a stirring 2-1 victory at Roker Park, Sunderland, and from then on there was no looking back as Kevin Keegan's men cruised towards the title, never relinquishing top spot. United won the title on an emotional night at Blundell Park, Grimsby, and finished the season in cavalier style by beating Leicester City 7-1 with an incredible display of fluid attacking football, David Kelly and Andy Cole both hitting hat-tricks in a game they led 6-0 at half-time. The Premier League awaited the re-born Newcastle United.

2009/10
Manager: Chris Hughton

A final-day defeat at Villa Park in May 2009 had condemned United to Championship football and with pre-season results not being great – a humiliating 6-1 defeat at League One Orient for example – no-one quite knew what to expect. A draw on the opening day at fellow newly-relegated West Brom was a decent result for United and, when they followed that up with five straight wins, the United faithful dared to dream of a quick return to the Premier League. A shaky spell followed but, driven on by the likes of Kevin Nolan, Alan Smith and Steve Harper, United put together a 15-game unbeaten run from mid-October to February. Then, after losing at Derby, the next 17 games brought 13 wins and four draws and... bingo! United were promoted with six games to play and had the Championship wrapped up with three to play on a fabulous away day for players and fans alike at Plymouth.

Promotion Season Summaries

| | | Pl | Home | | | Goals | | Away | | | Goals | | Pts | Pos | Seasons in Second Tier |
			W	D	L	F	A	W	D	L	F	A			
1897/98	D2	30	14	0	1	43	10	7	3	5	21	22	45	2	5
1947/48	D2	42	18	1	2	46	13	6	7	8	26	28	56	2	7
1964/65	D2	42	16	4	1	50	16	8	5	8	31	29	57	1	4
1983/84	D2	42	16	2	3	51	18	8	6	7	34	35	80	3	6
1992/93	D1	46	16	6	1	58	15	13	3	7	34	23	96	1	4
2009/10	CH	46	18	5	0	56	13	12	7	4	34	22	102	1	1

SPOT THE DIFFERENCE

Can you spot the ten differences in this match between Newcastle and Southampton?

Answers on page 62

Newcastle United   **27**

UNITED'S EUROPEAN INFLUENCE

ICELAND

SWEDEN

FINLAND

NORWAY

RUSSIA

ESTONIA

LATVIA

Peter Lovenkrands

LITHUANIA

DENMARK

UNITED KINGDOM

Didi Hamann

BELARUS

IRELAND

NETHERLANDS

POLAND

GERMANY

BELGIUM

Pavel Srnicek

LUXEMBOURG

CZECH REP.

UKRAINE

Philippe Albert

Marc Hottiger

SLOVAKIA

MOLDOVA

LIECHTENSTEIN

AUSTRIA

FRANCE

SWITZERLAND

HUNGARY

SLOVENIA

ROMANIA

David Ginola

CROATIA

Temuri Ketsbaia

Giuseppe Rossi

BOSNIA AND HERZ.

SERBIA

GEORG

MONTENEGRO

BULGARIA

Emre Belozoglu

MACEDONIA

SPAIN

ITALY

ALBANIA

PORTUGAL

TURKEY

GREECE

Nikos Dabizas

MALTA

CYPRUS

Up until the end of the 2015/16 season, 64 non-British/Irish players from Europe have turned out for United in the Premier League era, not all of them successfully we might add. Nowadays, there is still a big contingent of continental European players at St. James' Park, as there has been throughout the last decade. Excluding the last few seasons, and taking just one player from each country, this feature looks at some of those who became popular figures on Tyneside.

Philippe Albert – Belgium

Born: Bouillon, Belgium on 10th August 1967
Played: 1994 – 1999
Debut: v Leicester City (H), 21st August 1994
Appearances: 138
Goals: 12
International Caps: 41

Nikos Dabizas – Greece

Born: Ptolemaida, Greece on 3rd August 1973
Played: 1998 – 2004
Debut: v Coventry City (H), 14th March 1998
Appearances: 176
Goals: 13
International Caps: 70

Cool and confident on the ball, Philippe was one of Belgium's stand-out performers at the 1994 World Cup in the USA and shortly after he duly became a United player. Philippe was to become a cult-hero on Tyneside with his stylish play endearing him to the Geordies, who loved to see him striding forward from the heart of the defence. He had an exquisite left foot and much of United's passing game started from his vision at the back, where he fitted perfectly into Kevin Keegan's Entertainers side. Dangerous at free-kicks and corners, and possessing a venomous shot, he was twice a Premier League runner-up with United. Philippe will always be remembered for his delightful chip over Peter Schmeichel in the famous 5-0 drubbing of Manchester United in October 1996. The popular and unassuming Belgian often returns to Tyneside, sometimes on television punditry duties, where he is always received with genuine warmth and affection.

A rugged, uncompromising centre-half who joined United from Greek giants Olympiakos. Nikos would go on to wear the black-and-white shirt for the next six seasons with distinction, displaying pride and passion in bucket-loads and leading by example with whole-hearted, committed displays. Shortly after he signed, Nikos gave a commanding performance in the FA Cup semi-final victory over Sheffield United at Old Trafford that saw United reach Wembley for the first time in 22 years. A favourite of Sir Bobby Robson, Nikos was capable of grabbing a goal or two at the other end of the park where he was particularly dangerous at set plays when the ball was flighted into the penalty area. One of the highlights of his career on Tyneside was when he scored the winner for United at the Stadium of Light in February 2002. Nikos appeared in two FA Cup finals for United and also had the honour of skippering his country on a number of occasions.

Emre Belozoglu – Turkey

Born: Istanbul, Turkey on 7th September 1980
Played: 2005 – 2008
Debut: v Deportivo La Coruna (H), 3rd August 2005
Appearances: 80
Goals: 6
International Caps: 91

David Ginola – France

Born: Gassin, France on 25th January 1967
Played: 1995 – 1997
Debut: v Coventry City (H), 19th August 1995
Appearances: 76
Goals: 7
International Caps: 17

Small in stature but well-built, Emre was a noted footballer on the European scene when he moved to the North East as a 24-year-old from Milan giants Internazionale during the summer of 2005. Appreciated by manager Graeme Souness, a fan of Turkish football from his own days in that country, Emre was a playmaker who had the ability from the centre of the park to create chances for the forward players and turn matches on their head. Emre was a celebrated name in his home city of Istanbul, where he was dubbed the 'Maradona of the Bosporus'. Another United player who would captain his country, he had excellent technical ability and was a dead-ball expert too – witness his stunning free-kick winner against Sunderland at St. James' Park in October 2005. His left foot was as good as any who wore a United shirt in the modern era, following in the footsteps as such schemers as Terry Hibbitt, Tommy Craig and Scott Sellars.

One of the Entertainers of the Kevin Keegan era and an outstanding talent who set United's fanatical Toon Army alight after joining Keegan's side from Paris St Germain. A virtuoso of the highest quality, he had immaculate balance and poise, was two-footed, and during the 1995/96 season he delivered the goods with entertainment to boot. Able to bamboozle every defender in the land, Ginola's wing play was exceptional. A pin-up star too, Ginola was a rare talent who thrilled supporters on both sides of the Channel. A flamboyant star with style and match-winning ability, his second season on Tyneside didn't quite live up to his first and in July 1997 he took his talents off to Tottenham, before also appearing for Aston Villa and Everton. It was on Tyneside though that he was at his peak as he made a huge impact on English football, but sadly he never really made his mark with the French national team.

Didi Hamann – Germany

Born: Waldassen, Germany on 27th August 1973
Played: 1998 – 1999
Debut: v Charlton Athletic (H), 15th August 1998
Appearances: 31
Goals: 5
International Caps: 59

Marc Hottiger – Switzerland

Born: Lausanne, Switzerland on 7th November 1967
Played: 1994 – 1996
Debut: v Leicester City (A), 21st August 1994
Appearances: 54
Goals: 2
International Caps: 63

Part of the Germany squad at the 1998 World Cup in France, Didi was one of United's headline purchases by Kenny Dalglish prior to the start of the 1998/99 season. The 24-year-old was an established star in his homeland when he moved to England to become United's first-ever German import. Tall and slender, he quickly adapted to the rigours of the Premier League – he was a midfielder of quality and a most effective player, able to hit accurate long and short passes and with an engine to last the full 90 minutes. Didi was a top-class player but didn't always catch the eye of Ruud Gullit, who had replaced Dalglish only days after the start of the new campaign. At the end of his first season on Tyneside, where he played in the FA Cup Final against Manchester United, he moved on to Liverpool where he enjoyed a successful seven-year career. Well respected but not a Geordie hero, he was famed for scoring the last competitive goal at the 'old' Wembley in September 2000.

Cultured right-back who impressed for Switzerland in the 1994 World Cup in the USA, before completing his move to United for what was a bargain fee for an international defender. Indeed, he captained his country and even scored the goal against Italy which secured qualification for the Swiss in the Finals. On Tyneside, Marc showed a calm attitude and his ability to link with the attack in the modern wing-back style caused opponents much consternation down the right flank, especially during the 1994/95 season when United finished in a very commendable sixth place. He scored twice for United, once at Stamford Bridge, but much more memorably in the FA Cup Third Round replay at Blackburn in January 1995, when he rifled in a long-range strike to help set up United's 2-1 victory – Lee Clark grabbing the winner. Good friends with Peter Beardsley, who was one of his biggest fans, Marc also had a spell with Everton before returning to his homeland.

Temuri Ketsbaia – Georgia

Born: Gali, Georgia on 18th March 1968
Played: 1997 – 2000
Debut: v Sheffield Wednesday (H), 9th August 1997
Appearances: 109
Goals: 14
International Caps: 31

Peter Lovenkrands – Denmark

Born: Horsholm, Denmark on 29th January 1980
Played: 2009 – 2012
Debut: v Manchester City (A), 28th January 2009
Appearances: 85
Goals: 29
International Caps: 22

A cult figure on Tyneside, Temuri, who has recently taken over as manager of Greek side AEK Athens, arrived on Tyneside from the aforementioned side where he was already recognised as one of the Greek league's top players. Already an established Georgian International, United took advantage of the 'Bosman' ruling to land Temuri on a free transfer. With a football brain and non-stop engine, coupled with an attacking instinct from his midfield role, he was fast on and off the ball and his weaving, penetrating runs gave his side a much needed impetus. Not always an automatic choice, he made plenty of game-changing appearances from the bench but he was without doubt a popular character on Tyneside. After scoring a crucial goal against Bolton in January 1998, he embarked on what is now known as a 'Ketsbaia', namely kicking the advertising board at the Gallowgate End of the ground in pure frustration. Temuri played in both the 1998 and 1999 FA Cup Finals.

Hugely popular striker who didn't join United until he was 28-years old, but by then he had already been capped 20 times for Denmark. A former Glasgow Rangers player, where he won the Premier League and Scottish Cup, he wasn't big or muscular but was a forward with pace who ran the channels. Peter had a natural goal-poacher's instinct around the box and often played as the supporting striker where he proved very effective. During United's Championship-winning campaign of 2009/10, Peter scored 13 valuable goals in 29 appearances for the Magpies. The Dane almost joined the Geordies back in 2000 when Bobby Robson tried to bring him to St. James' Park but he opted for Scotland instead before moving on to Schalke 04 in Germany. Peter scored some tremendous goals in a black-and-white shirt, notably against Manchester United at Gallowgate and he also grabbed a memorable FA Cup hat-trick against Plymouth in January 2010.

Giuseppe Rossi – Italy

Born: New Jersey, USA on 1st February 1987
Played: 2006 – 2007
Debut: v Fulham (H), 9th September 2006
Appearances: 13
Goals: 1
International Caps: 30

Pavel Srnicek – Czech Republic

Born: Ostrava, Czech Republic on 10th March 1968
Played: 1990 – 1998 & 2006 – 2007
Debut: v Sheffield Wednesday (H), 17th April 1991
Appearances: 190
Goals: 0
International Caps: 49

USA-born of Italian parents, Giuseppe was brought to St. James' Park by Glenn Roeder on a loan deal from Manchester United. Just 19 at the time, United were short in the forward department with Alan Shearer having just retired and Michael Owen injured. Small, compact but skilful and quick, the young Italian impressed the fans with his style of play, commitment and ability to play good football – good traits in anyone's books. Favouring a role on the left, alongside a main striker, he was an Owen-like predator, quick to take a snap-shot although he managed only one goal for United during his time on Tyneside. After returning to Old Trafford he ultimately moved on to Villarreal in Spain where he helped his new side reach the Champions League. He was soon capped by Italy and even went on to captain the Azzurri in 2010. It was a case of what might have been for the striker at United, a good player that maybe slipped through their hands.

'Pavel is a Geordie' says it all about the popular goalkeeper who so sadly died on 29th December 2015 after suffering a heart attack nine days earlier whilst out jogging. He arrived on Tyneside from Banik Ostrava in January 1991, brought to the club by Jim Smith. Initially, he made a handful of reserve appearances, impressing enough for United to complete a permanent transfer. Pavel had begun his playing career with army sides Dukla Tabor and Dukla Prague and was capped at U21 level by the Czech Republic. A brilliant shot-stopper and good with his feet too, he made his United debut under Ossie Ardiles but flourished under Kevin Keegan where he was a mainstay of the 1992/93 Championship-winning team. His time at Gallowgate drew to a close in 1997 following the arrival of Shay Given. Pavel embraced the Geordie culture and was delighted to return to the club for a brief spell during the 2006/07 season. A regular visitor to Tyneside before his death, Pavel will always have a place in the hearts of the United fans.

THE ALDER SWEENEY MEMORIAL GARDEN

NEWCASTLE UNITED

IN MEMORY OF ALL NEWCASTLE UNITED SUPPORTERS WHO ARE NO LONGER WITH US

Memorial Garden

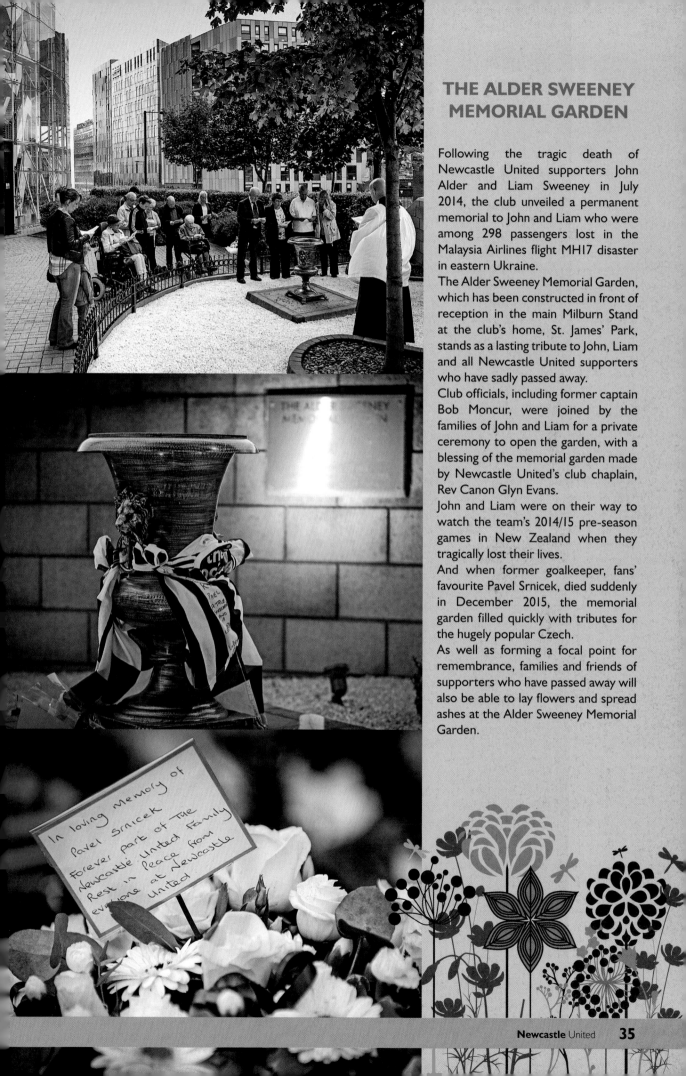

THE ALDER SWEENEY MEMORIAL GARDEN

Following the tragic death of Newcastle United supporters John Alder and Liam Sweeney in July 2014, the club unveiled a permanent memorial to John and Liam who were among 298 passengers lost in the Malaysia Airlines flight MH17 disaster in eastern Ukraine.

The Alder Sweeney Memorial Garden, which has been constructed in front of reception in the main Milburn Stand at the club's home, St. James' Park, stands as a lasting tribute to John, Liam and all Newcastle United supporters who have sadly passed away.

Club officials, including former captain Bob Moncur, were joined by the families of John and Liam for a private ceremony to open the garden, with a blessing of the memorial garden made by Newcastle United's club chaplain, Rev Canon Glyn Evans.

John and Liam were on their way to watch the team's 2014/15 pre-season games in New Zealand when they tragically lost their lives.

And when former goalkeeper, fans' favourite Pavel Srnicek, died suddenly in December 2015, the memorial garden filled quickly with tributes for the hugely popular Czech.

As well as forming a focal point for remembrance, families and friends of supporters who have passed away will also be able to lay flowers and spread ashes at the Alder Sweeney Memorial Garden.

CUP FINAL HEROES

In their illustrious history, Newcastle United have appeared in 15 major Cup Finals; 13 FA Cup, one League Cup and one European Fairs Cup. In this feature we focus on some of the United heroes who have helped bring the much sought-after silverware back to Tyneside.

Albert Shepherd 1910

A centre-forward who left his mark in United's history books in spectacular fashion. Shepherd led the line with lightning pace and netted twice during the 1910 FA Cup final win over Barnsley, including the first penalty in a cup final. In all games he found the net 92 times in just 123 appearances.

Stan Seymour 1924

One of the most distinguished names in Newcastle's history, Stan dominated the outside left position in a black-and-white shirt for eight seasons as a goal-scoring winger of merit. Linking well with the likes of Tom McDonald and Hughie Gallacher, he scored in only the second Cup Final at Wembley and won the League Championship three years later.

Jack Allan 1932

Tyneside born and bred, Jack was an aggressive leader of the line who found some eye-catching form as the Magpies set their sights on Wembley in 1932. He struck seven FA Cup goals that season, including two in the final as United beat Arsenal in the famous 'Over the line Final'. Highly effective, Jack returned a goal every second game for United.

Jackie Milburn 1951, 1952, 1955

"Wor Jackie" held Newcastle United's goalscoring record until 2006 when Alan Shearer surpassed his tremendous feat. Born in Ashington, local boy Jackie became the archetypal Geordie hero as his goalscoring ability took Tyneside by storm.

Widely recognised as one of the best in the business, he scored many breath-taking goals as he won three FA Cup winner's medals.

Bobby Mitchell 1951, 1952, 1955

Bobby was one of the darlings of the Newcastle crowd during the immediate post-war years. Known throughout football as 'Bobby Dazzler', he was famed for his immaculate ball control and wing wizardry and he scored many an important goal for United. He thrilled the United crowd with his magical footwork and ball skills in a 13-year Gallowgate career.

George Robledo 1951, 1952

A deadly goal-getter, Chilean-born George formed an outstanding forward line with Jackie Milburn and Bobby Mitchell, a trio that scared defences up and down the country. George was a grafter too, working hard for the team but was lethal in front of goal whenever an opportunity came his way. Scored the winner in the 1952 final.

George Hannah 1955

Possessing lovely ball skills, George was a joy to watch. He had deceiving pace and was slick on the ball with quicksilver movement. Not always an automatic choice, he found his best form between 1952 and 1955 and in the third cup final victory, over Manchester City in 1955, he played a starring role for the Magpies, scoring the crucial third goal.

Benny Arentoft 1969

A diminutive but stocky Danish midfield worker, Ben excelled in a close-marking role during United's first assault on the European football scene in 1968/69. An astute player who read the game well, Preben, to give him his full name, scored the crucial second goal in Hungary which really knocked the stuffing out of the hosts as United went on to lift the trophy.

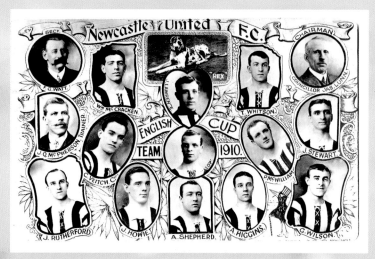

Alan Foggon 1969

Alan made his debut at 17, trendy with long, flowing hair he had a somewhat untidy appearance on the field, playing with his socks down and shirt outside his shorts. But he had ability too, and his pacy, direct running at defences was his major asset. His best moment came when he superbly rifled in the third goal against Ujpest in Hungary.

Bob Moncur 1969

Captain of United and Scotland, Bobby is best remembered for lifting the Inter Cities Fairs Cup in 1969, after the black-and-whites beat the Hungarians Ujpest Dozsa 6 – 2 in the two-legged final. Remarkably, Moncur also helped himself to three goals in the final. A rugged and determined player, he marshalled the United backline superbly during his fourteen years on Tyneside.

United arrive home with the FA Cup in 1955

For the record, the full list of finals reads as follows:

FA CUP

14 April 1905
Newcastle United 0–2 Aston Villa
Venue: Crystal Palace   Attendance: 101,117

21 April 1906
Newcastle United 0–1 Aston Villa
Venue: Crystal Palace   Attendance: 75,609

25 April 1908
Newcastle United 1–3 Wolverhampton Wanderers
United Scorer: Jimmy Howie 73
Venue: Crystal Palace   Attendance: 74,967

23 April 1910
Newcastle United 1–1 Barnsley
United Scorer: Jack Rutherford 83
Venue: Crystal Palace   Attendance: 76,980

28 April 1910 (Replay)
Newcastle United 2–0 Barnsley
United Scorers: Albert Shepherd 2 (51 & 65 pen)
Venue: Everton   Attendance: 69,364

22 April 1911
Newcastle United 0–0 Bradford City
Venue: Crystal Palace   Attendance: 69,800

26 April 1911 (Replay)
Newcastle United 0–1 Bradford City
Venue: Old Trafford   Attendance: 66,646

26 April 1924
Newcastle United 2–0 Aston Villa
United Scorers: Stan Seymour 83, Neil Harris 86
Venue: Wembley   Attendance: 91,695

23 April 1932
Newcastle United 2–1 Arsenal
United Scorers: Jack Allan 2 (38 & 72)
Venue: Wembley   Attendance: 92,298

28 April 1951
Newcastle United 2–0 Blackpool
United Scorers: Jackie Milburn 2 (50 & 55)
Venue: Wembley   Attendance: 100,000

3 May 1952
Newcastle United 1–0 Arsenal
United Scorer: George Robledo 84
Venue: Wembley   Attendance: 100,000

7 May 1955
Newcastle United 3–1 Manchester City
United Scorers:
Jackie Milburn 1, Bobby Mitchell 53, George Hannah 58
Venue: Wembley   Attendance: 100,000

4 May 1974
Newcastle United 0–3 Liverpool
Venue: Wembley   Attendance: 100,000

16 May 1998
Newcastle United 0–2 Arsenal
Venue: Wembley   Attendance: 79,183

22 May 1999
Newcastle United 0–2 Manchester United
Venue: Wembley   Attendance: 79,101

LEAGUE CUP

28 February 1976
Newcastle United 1–2 Manchester City
United Scorer: Alan Gowling 35
Venue: Wembley   Attendance: 100,000

INTER CITIES FAIRS CUP

29 May 1969
Newcastle United 3–0 Ujpest Dozsa
United Scorers: Bob Moncur 2 (63 & 71), Jimmy Scott 84
Venue: St. James' Park   Attendance: 59,234

11 June 1969
Newcastle United 3–2 Ujpest Dozsa
United Scorers:
Bob Moncur 46, Ben Arentoft 53, Alan Foggon 68
Venue: Megyeri Uti Stadion Attendance: 34,000

United have also appeared in a number of secondary cup finals, such as the Texaco Cup and Anglo Italian Cup, competitions they won in the mid 1970s.

NEWCASTLE UNITED CROSSWORD

We hope you enjoy our Newcastle United crossword. Simply solve all the clues and then insert your answers into the grid. It's a fun challenge which will definitely test your knowledge of all things Newcastle United!

ACROSS

4 Sadly missed former Czech goalkeeper. (7)
5 Charlie, Cup-winning full-back from 1951. (5)
8 Joined United from Manchester United in 2004. (4)
11 French wide man 2011-2016. (7)
12 Hungarian centre-half from 2009/10. (5)
13 Italian full-back, now at Inter Milan. (6)
16 Turkey international. (4)
17 Club captain from 2009/10 Championship season. (5)
18 Geordie phrase Whey ___. (3)

DOWN

1 French winger from Sir Bobby's team. (6)
2 Five-time World Cup winners. (7)
3 Big Dunc. (8)
6 Scott with the cultured left foot from the 1990s. (7)
7 Former 'keeper, now a Saint. (7)
8 Nigerian left back. (8)
9 England midfielder signed from Chelsea in 2005. (6)
10 Scored against Spurs in May 2016. (6)
14 Chilean international. (5)
15 On-loan French striker in 2013/14. (4)

Answers on page 62

RAFA BENITEZ
HIS CAREER IN PICTURES

Prowling the touch line at Valencia's Mestalla Stadium

2003/04 making it a double-winning season for the 'Los Che'.

Benitez moved to England in the summer of 2004 with the highlight of his six years on Merseyside being the lifting of the European Cup (Champions League) for the fifth time in the club's history – beating AC Milan on penalties in Istanbul in 2005. Liverpool also won the FA Cup in 2006 and reached the final of the Champions League again in 2007. His best finishing position in the Premier League was a runners-up spot achieved in 2008/09.

Bringing the Champions League trophy back to Liverpool

Madrid-born Rafael Benitez's first coaching role was with Real Madrid 'B' from 1993-95 before brief managerial spells at Real Valladolid and Osauna. He then spent two seasons at Extremadura during which time he lead them back to the Primera Division in 1997. He moved on to Tenerife and won promotion with them too in his only season at the club in 2001.

By then his reputation was growing in Spain and he was appointed manager of Valencia in 2001, where he brought the La Liga title to the Mestalla in 2001/2 and again in 2003/4. The UEFA Cup was also won in

Rafa and Javier Zanetti with the Supercoppa Italiano

He left Liverpool in the summer of 2010 to move to Inter Milan, but left the Italian giants midway through the 2010/11 season, despite winning the Supercoppa Italiana and FIFA Club World Cup. It was back to England for Rafael in November 2012 when he was appointed interim manager of Chelsea in place of Roberto Di Matteo. He guided Chelsea to a third-place finish and also won the Europa League for the Blues that season.

Rafa with the Europa League trophy won with Chelsea in 2013.

Real Madrid's Luka Modric listening intently to Rafa

With Jose Mourinho coming into Chelsea on a permanent basis for the 2013/14 season, Benitez returned to Italy where he spent two years at Napoli, winning the Coppa Italia and Supercoppa Italiana, before taking on the post of Head Coach at Real Madrid in June 2015. Despite being in third place in La Liga in January 2016, and guiding his side to the knockout stages of the Champions League, Benitez was dismissed by the Spaniards.

Newcastle United appointed Benitez in March 2016 but, despite being unable to save the Magpies from relegation, he decided to remain at the club with the sole focus of restoring the club's top flight status and then building the club back to a position of strength in the Premier League.

Benitez is the only manager in history to have won the UEFA Cup, UEFA Super League, UEFA Champions League and FIFA Club World Cup. He was also named UEFA Manager of the Year in 2003/4 and 2004/5.

Rafa with Napoli striker Gonzalo Higuain

And back to the present - in the technical area at St. James' Park

DID YOU KNOW?

In our popular series 'Did You Know' we've found even more wonderful facts and figures about Newcastle United.

1880/81
Newcastle Rangers play the first ever game of football at St. James' Park.

1893/94
Willie Thompson scores United's first Football League hat-trick as he nets three in United's 6-0 win over Woolwich Arsenal.

1899/1900
Fog causes the abandonment of United's home game with Glossop; United were trailing 3–2 when the game ended after 72 minutes.

1900/01
The derby match with Sunderland at St. James' Park is abandoned without a ball being kicked due to over-crowding with 45,000 inside and many thousands more outside.

1904/05
United are watched by the biggest attendance ever to see the Magpies; 101,117 at Crystal Palace for the FA Cup Final.

1908/09
Bill Appleyard nets nine times for United, a club record, in the 14–1 friendly win in Anglesey over Beaumaris.

1921/22
Jimmy Lawrence keeps his 173rd and final clean sheet for United, a club record.

1926/27
Billy Hampson becomes United's oldest player at 42 years and 225 days at Birmingham.

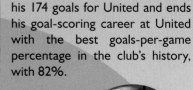

1929/30
Hughie Gallacher scores the last of his 174 goals for United and ends his goal-scoring career at United with the best goals-per-game percentage in the club's history, with 82%.

1931/32
United record their highest FA Cup win, 9–0 over Southport in a Fourth Round second replay played at Hillsborough; Jimmy Richardson grabbed a hat-trick.

1933/34
United beat Liverpool 9–2 at St. James' Park, seven of the goals – including a hat-trick from Sam Weaver – coming in the second half, a club record.

1937/38
Albert Stubbins makes his United debut at Luton. He scored six goals in 30 games for United before war intervened when he notched a further 231 goals in 188 games, a remarkable record.

1949/50
George Robledo becomes the first Newcastle United player to represent his country at the World Cup Finals, appearing in the game against England in the Maracana Stadium in Rio, Brazil.

1950/51
Jackie Milburn scores in all six rounds of the FA Cup as United lift the trophy at Wembley.

1951/52
Winston Churchill, for the first time, presents the trophy to the FA Cup winners at Wembley, on this occasion Newcastle United and captain Joe Harvey after their 1-0 win over Arsenal.

1955/56
Jackie Milburn hits his 23rd FA Cup goal for United against Fulham, a club record.

1959/60
United fans are treated to ten goals at St. James' Park and seven of them end up in the back of the Manchester United net including a Len White hat-trick.

1961/62
United lift the FA Youth Cup for the first time, defeating Wolves 2–1 on aggregate.

1968/69
United beat Real Zarogoza 2–1 on Tyneside, but the Fairs Cup tie finishes 4–4 on aggregate. The Magpies take advantage of the away goals rule for the first time and the Spaniards are eliminated.

1971/72
United come up against the legendary Pele as United meet

the Brazilian outfit Santos in an end-of-season friendly in Hong Kong. Santos win 4–2 with John Tudor and Tony Green scoring for the Magpies.

1972/73
United win the Anglo-Italian Cup, defeating Fiorentina 2–1 in Florence with goals from Superchi (og) and David Craig.

1973/74
Malcolm Macdonald scores twice in dramatic fashion as United beat Burnley 2–0 in the FA Cup Semi-Final at Hillsborough.

1977/78
The famous Leazes End is no more as, following the home 2–2 draw with Manchester City in March, the roof is removed from the stand, much to the chagrin of United's vocal and vociferous Leazes Enders.

1991/92
Kevin Keegan takes charge of United for the first time, a 3–0 home win over Bristol City.

1993/94
Newcastle field an all-English line-up in the fixture against Liverpool (1993).

1995/96
A re-modelled St. James' Park is completed for the first game of the season against Coventry.

1996/97
Alan Shearer hits a 13-minute hat-trick, including a last-minute winner, as United storm back from 3–1 down to beat the Foxes 4–3 at St. James' Park.

2004/05
United finished with just eight men in the 3–0 home defeat to Aston Villa, with three red cards being shown by referee Barry Knight.

2007/08
United are watched by the highest attendance to see them play in a League fixture; 75,965 at Manchester United.

2009/10
Steve Harper keeps his 21st clean sheet of the season, a club record.

2010/11
United trail Arsenal 4–0 at half time at St. James' Park, but make a remarkable recovery to draw the game 4–4 – Cheick Tiote scoring in the 87th minute to level things up.

2011/12
The Sir Bobby Robson Statue is unveiled by his widow Lady Elsie at St. James' Park, prior to United's home fixture with Manchester City.

2013/14
Tim Krul appears as a 120th minute substitute against Costa Rica in Salvador, Brazil, and saves two of five penalties as the Dutch progress to the semi-finals of the World Cup, 4–3 on penalties after a 0–0 draw.

2015/16
Aleksandar Mitrovic's goal against Tottenham on the final day of the season was the 1,000th Premier League goal of the season.

United in the Community

Newcastle United Foundation is the official charity of Newcastle United Football Club. It uses the local passion for football to inspire, encourage learning and promote healthy lifestyles, making a real difference to the lives of children, young people and families in the North East region.

Through its health, community, education and coaching programmes the Foundation has worked with almost 50,000 people across Newcastle, Gateshead, North Tyneside and Northumberland in the last year.

Here are a few pictures of some of the projects from last season together with a number of other activities and events, including linking up with commercial partners, which the players were involved with as part of their commitment to support the local community.

Jack Colback and Papiss Cisse dropped in at one of the regular Newcastle United Disabled Supporters Association's functions at St. James' Park, mingling with all the guests young and old. Every photo was signed and every picture request happily obliged. Here Jack is pictured with NUDSA's Stephen Miller, a multiple Paralympic gold medallist. Chancel Mbemba, Florian Thauvin and manager Rafa Benitez also attended NUDSA events during the year.

All members of the Newcastle United first-team squad visit the local children's hospitals at Christmas time. Armed with presents and goodwill, they aim to bring a little cheer to the children from the region who are unfortunate enough to be hospitalised at this time of year.

The Royal Victoria Infirmary, which houses the Great North Children's Hospital, is the main beneficiary of the visit and they also receive a cash donation from the players. Pictured are Rolando Aarons and Papiss Cisse.

Ayoze Perez was a guest of honour at the annual Bravehearts of the North East awards. 30 children received awards, as well as gifts, from Perez and BBC Look North presenter Carol Malia. Bravehearts is a charity which recognises the courage and bravery in children of the region, many of whom have undergone major operations at the Royal Victoria Infirmary. Ayoze said, "I was amazed at the bravery of the children, they were all smiling and that is a great lesson for us all."

Magpies duo Rob Elliot and Jamaal Lascelles supported the 20th anniversary of Show Racism the Red Card (SRtRC). Over 100 school children attended a question-and-answer session with former Newcastle players Olivier Bernard, Steve Howey and John Anderson. SRtRC was founded in 1996 with the help of United goalkeeper Shaka Hislop, who attended the first SRtRC roadshow with Les Ferdinand. Rob Elliot said: "It's great for Show Racism the Red Card to educate local kids and make people aware about the whole issue around racism."

Mike Williamson visited a Newcastle United Foundation Building Futures session, which is supported by the Postcode Community Trust, and uses football to inspire young people to reach their full potential. The support from the Postcode Community Trust means that over the year the project will engage with over 500 children with disabilities at 32 SEN schools and over 1200 young people through Kicks. The project aims to encourage communities to feel proud of their local area and build a sense of community between people from different backgrounds.

In a ground-breaking project supported by Port of Tyne, Newcastle United Foundation and Sunderland AFC's Foundation of Light brought together young people from north and south of the River Tyne to break down barriers and work on exciting business challenges. The project involved more than 100 young people, assisted by Rolando Aarons and Wes Brown, who were challenged to develop an advertising campaign, whilst also increasing their confidence and self-esteem through gaining skills in business and enterprise, life skills and personal and social development skills.

Over 300 families attended one of Newcastle United Foundation's annual Family Football Celebration events, supported by The Big Lottery Fund, with special guest Rob Elliot at St. James' Park. Family Football, delivered at schools, uses the power of football to bring families together to enjoy learning. The sessions are split into one-hour learning in the classroom and one hour of activity. Last season the Foundation delivered 31 Family Football Courses in local schools and community venues involving over 1300 people.

Siem de Jong made a special visit to an inspiring initiative led by the Prince's Trust, in partnership with Newcastle United Foundation, which is helping young people boost their career prospects and become the next generation of sports coaches. He joined youngsters aged 16-24 at Gateshead Redheugh FC for a session of the Get Started programme, which is delivered by the Foundation.

The young people, who are all unemployed or not in training or education, are learning about prospective careers in sports coaching and how they can volunteer in their local community to gain coaching experience.

North-East car dealership Pulman Volkswagen strengthened its commercial relationship with Newcastle United by becoming one of the club's Platinum Partners. Gini Wijnaldum and Ayoze Perez were in Durham to support the partnership which has seen Pulman, one of the most respected and trusted businesses in the region, supplying cars to the club from its extensive fleet of brand new Volkswagens since 2009. Newcastle United will continue to benefit from a range of commercial and hospitality opportunities at St. James' Park.

The inaugural Newcastle United Foundation 1892 Cup took place at the Magpies' Academy in July and featured 128 football-mad youngsters from eight local primary schools; each with a boys' and a girls' team. And thanks to official club partner Sports Direct, they were all fully kitted out with a new 2016/17 home kit. United manager Rafa Benítez was at the tournament to hand out the awards and said: "We were very pleased to have hosted this very special tournament and to bring the community and our young supporters closer to the club."

WORD SEARCH

Answers on page 62

Answer the questions below to find the 20 words that are hidden in the grid. Words can go horizontally, vertically and diagonally in all eight directions.

```
R C G L T N Q K K C X G S K K J C J
D P H I G H B U R Y A L W R L L L B
Y N Y A U G U R U L V G H N E R M Y
E R C W L L D C L R A Y T M T V Z M
L P R C R E U A B N E K C E B X O A
S X L R F Z C D I L M Z R G X Z S R
N Z M V T H R T Q R O T R R D F D A
R L C K E M N N P N H O F N X F N C
A S I R P E N K A W B T Y K E E A A
B T T N G N D L D S V R K T G Y R N
Z B E R E R O G O P J L V V D E K A
Y Q A L A S M N E Y V T R Q E N N J
F R L P Y C M P T R Y L K J L O E Z
B P M Z T G H A X G M L N L T O V B
T A K K L C R A N D V A W W U R O R
L K R N N T H A N H K K N V O D L M
T L M I L B U R N Z N X K Y R K T H
N R P T P X L C T O T T E N H A M N
```

1 League One Play-off winners in 2016 ... (8)

2 United's Peruvian, Nobby ... (6)

3 Wor Jackie ... (7)

4 Current World Champions ... (7)

5 Brazil National Stadium ... (8)

6 The one and only Sir Bobby ...(6)

7 German World Cup captain Franz ... (11)

8 League Two Team Plymouth ... (6)

9 Wayne from 2009/10 season ... (9)

10 Coloccini's country ... (9)

11 Arsenal's old stadium ... (8)

12 Our Dane Peter ... (11)

13 Scotland Manager Gordon ... (8)

14 United's first Euro opponents, Dutch side ... (9)

15 The legendary Hughie ... (9)

16 Hosted and won the first World Cup ... (7)

17 Frank formerly of Chelsea ... (7)

18 Comic book star, Roy of the ... (5)

19 United did the double over them in 2015/16 ... (9)

20 Name for Assistant Referee ... (8)

TOP TEN GOALS 2015/16

It wasn't the best season for goals if you were a follower of Newcastle United, with only 48 being scored in all competitions, but that doesn't mean the ten we have selected here aren't up with the best we've seen in recent years, both at St. James' Park and on the road.

And if you had to choose the best? Well, take a pick from either Andros Townsend's stunning free-kick against Crystal Palace or, for pure drama, Aleksandar Mitrovic's equaliser against Sunderland.

Georginio Wijnaldum v Southampton (St. James' Park), 9/8/15

Hopes were high on Tyneside when Ronald Koeman's Saints arrived on Tyneside for the opening game of the season. Three minutes after half time, with the score tied at 1-1, United broke at pace down the right with Papiss Cisse setting Gabriel Obertan charging off down the wing. The Frenchman breezed past Matt Targett before supplying an inch-perfect first-time cross for debutant Wijnaldum to glance a header into the far corner of the Gallowgate net, past a helpless Maarten Stekelenburg.

Aleksandar Mitrovic v Norwich City (St. James' Park), 18/10/15

United had yet to win in the League and were leading 3-2 against a determined Canaries side when, midway through the second half, Daryl Janmaat won the ball deep in his own half before linking up with Ayoze Perez and Moussa Sissoko. The latter then hit a fabulous pass, dissecting the Norwich defence, which reached Mitrovic on the edge of the box. The Serb chested the ball down before hammering it in with his left foot in a manner reminiscent of the legendary Alan Shearer – remember his equaliser against Everton in December 2002?

Ayoze Perez v Tottenham Hotspur (White Hart Lane), 13/12/15

United were level with Tottenham as the game moved into the third minute of injury-time. Aleksandar Mitrovic, who had already scored the equaliser, nodded Gini Wijnaldum's flicked pass over Jan Verthonghen and into the Spurs box. Running out of space, and with Verthonghen breathing down his neck, Perez allowed the ball to roll off his chest and as it dropped he hit a powerful first-time right-footed shot past a stunned Hugo Lloris at the Park Lane End of the ground. Players and fans went ballistic.

Paul Dummett v Manchester United (St. James' Park), 12/1/16

The United defender doesn't score many but this was a classic strike, and a crucial one too. With time virtually up, and United trailing 3-2, Moussa Sissoko's right wing cross was cleared but Daryl Janmaat clipped it into the area and when the ball dropped on the edge of the box, Paul Dummett sprinted forward and lashed it into the roof of the Gallowgate End net via a slight Chris Smalling deflection that was past David de Gea before he could react. And, like his previous Gallowgate End goal against Liverpool, he celebrated wildly.

Georginio Wijnaldum v West Ham United (St. James' Park), 16/1/16

The Dutch midfielder had already scored eight goals for his new side, all incidentally coming at St. James' Park. Fifteen minutes in, and with United already a goal to the good, Jonjo Shelvey's exquisite 60-yard cross-field ball out to Daryl Janmaat on the United right was taken down at pace and the full back's cross picked out Wijnaldum who timed his run into the six-yard box perfectly to smash the ball past Adrian into the roof of the Gallowgate net. A great move deserving of a quality finish.

Aleksandar Mitrovic v Sunderland (St. James' Park), 20/3/16

Whisper it on Tyneside, but the Black Cats had won the last six derby matches on the trot and, with only seven minutes left on the clock at an increasingly anxious St. James' Park, a seventh was looming fast. Decisive action was needed to avoid another humiliation at the hands of United's arch-rivals. It came when Gini Wijnaldum jinked inside and out before crossing from the right flank for Aleksandar Mitrovic to head in at the Gallowgate End past Vito Mannone. Paroxysms of joy for the big Serb.

Andros Townsend v Southampton (St Mary's Stadium), 9/4/16

St. Mary's has not been a happy hunting ground for United in recent seasons and it was no different today. Needing at least a point to boost their survival chances, United were already three down when, with 25 minutes remaining, Andros Townsend cut inside from the right flank before unleashing a fierce left-foot drive that absolutely flew past Fraser Forster. A great strike, and his second for United, but regrettably too little too late for Rafa Benitez's side.

Vurnon Anita v Manchester City (St. James' Park), 19/4/16

United were feeling hard done by after Sergio Aguero had put the visitors ahead from a clearly offside position early in the game, so the equaliser was greeted with great delight. Just past the half-hour, and with referee Kevin Friend playing a good advantage, Moussa Sissoko spread the ball out to versatile Dutchman Vurnon Anita on the right wing. After an excellent first touch, he cut inside Aleksandar Kolarov and superbly curled a left-footed effort beyond Joe Hart and in off the post at the Leazes End.

Andros Townsend v Crystal Palace (St. James' Park), 30/4/16

Alan Pardew was returning to St. James' Park for the first time since leaving Tyneside midway through the 2014/15 season but it was a game United simply had to win. Scoreless just before the hour, Andros Townsend's charge down the United right was illegally halted by Scott Dann. With a curling cross into the crowded box looking likely, Townsend instead executed a left footed effort with precision and power that sailed beyond Wayne Hennessey before making the far side of the net bulge. A stupendous strike.

Rolando Aarons v Tottenham Hotspur (St. James' Park), 15/5/16

United were already relegated but who would have thought it on this incredible afternoon. The Magpies were already 3-1 up and were rampant against a Tottenham side who had come so close to Premier League glory. Following a short corner, Andros Townsend shot against the woodwork and when the ball was returned into the middle by Daryl Janmaat, it fell invitingly for substitute Rolando Aarons to react superbly, controlling it and firing incisively past Hugo Lloris before leaping into the crowd to celebrate.

UNITED during the WARS

Tommy Goodwill

The Football League began back in 1888 and has been played continuously since then bar having to break for two World War conflicts. War was declared in 1914 before the 1914/15 Football league season kicked off but, remarkably, football continued in England largely unaffected. As battles intensified, it was clear sport could not continue as normal. Spectators at St. James' Park often turned up in their forces uniforms, and injured soldiers were even seen in the crowds. United played their last game, for what would be more than four years, on 28 April 1915, a 3-0 home win over Aston Villa, which saw Tommy Goodwill (left) open the scoring for the Magpies. Sadly United's marksman that day would lose his life in the conflict in July 1916.

Football was suspended and players' contracts cancelled. Newcastle United were one of many clubs to bring down the shutters; the Magpies all but closing down during July 1915 before football returned to full swing after the Great War for the 1919/20 season. Jimmy Lawrence (below) kept goal in that last match against Villa and he pulled on the 'keeper's shirt once again at Arsenal when United opened the new season with a 1-0 win at Highbury. Given Lawrence is United's all-time record appearance holder (496 games), just imagine how many more games he would have clocked up if he hadn't missed four seasons of football. And note also, goalkeepers wore the same colour shirt as their outfield colleagues until there was a rule change in 1909.

Sadly the disruptions, and horrors, of war were to resurface in 1939 when the 1939/40 season was only three games old. United had lost their first two games but then hammered Swansea Town 8-1 at Gallowgate, the day before war was declared. It's unimaginable now that senior football all but closed down for seven years. Those three games were wiped from the record books, a shame for Ray Bowden who hit a hat-trick, but of course priorities now lay elsewhere.

Unlike during the Great War 25 years earlier, the government wanted the game to continue in some form and although there were restrictions on crowd numbers attending sporting events, war-time football was very popular and developed a regional structure with lots of friendly games organised too where clubs were able to play guest players. For United, Tom Finney and Stan Mortensen both represented United on occasions, players who would become huge post-war stars.

For United the real star of war-time football was the legendary Albert Stubbins. Born in 1919 in Wallsend,

Jimmy Lawrence

United line up ready for action in 1944, Stubbins is second left and Milburn far right.

Albert Stubbins

war broke out just when he would have been making his mark with United's first team. Despite that, in the war years, he hit an incredible 237 goals for the club in only 217 games. Stubbins (left) had a terrific turn of pace and loved running at defenders. He was England's best striker and was worshipped by the Geordie fans who were stunned when he left United for Liverpool in September 1946 in search of top-flight football. He has a connection with the music industry too, being featured as one of the faces on the cover of the Beatle's album 'Sergeant Pepper's Lonely Hearts Club Band'.

In 1945-46, with World War Two over, the national game returned to a semblance of familiarity. Regional Leagues continued but they were split north and south with a normal 42-match home and away programme (the top division was 22 teams back then until it was reduced to 20 in 1995/96). Crowds flocked back to stadiums all over the country and an average attendance of over 40,000 at Gallowgate saw United hit a century of goals, registering four or more goals in a game on 12 occasions during the season. The FA Cup was back too with the Third Round being played over two-legs for the only time

in its history. It's the only occasion that United won an FA Cup match (4-2) only to then exit the completion – a 3-0 second-leg loss sent Barnsley through to Round Four on a 5-4 aggregate.

Great United players of the 1950s, including the likes of Jackie Milburn and Bobby Cowell, made their debuts in war-time football and it certainly didn't do them any harm at all.

Newcastle meet Middlesbrough in a V.E. Day celebration match at St. James' Park.

Q AND A

JAMAAL LASCELLES

Boyhood Hero?
Rio Ferdinand.

Best footballing moment?
Being made club captain at Newcastle

Toughest opponent?
Sergio Aguero.

Team supported as a boy?
Arsenal.

Pre-match meal/Favourite food?
Porridge & Bananas/Mum's home cooking.

Any superstitions?
I prepare for each game the same every time.

Favourite current player?
Sergio Ramos.

Favourite other sports person?
Anthony Joshua.

Favourite stadium other than St. James' Park?
The Etihad (Manchester City).

What would you be if you weren't a footballer?
Basketball player (my favourite other sport).

Where did you go for your 2016 summer holiday?
Barbados.

What do you like in particular about the city of Newcastle?
The friendly people.

Favourite actor/actress?
Liam Neeson/Angelina Jolie.

Favourite TV show?
Game of Thrones.

Favourite music artist and last concert seen?
R & B, Future/Beyonce.

What do you like doing in your spare time?
Just relaxing at home and with friends.

Best friend in football?
Karl Darlow

Which three people would you invite round for dinner?
My friends.

What's the best thing about being a footballer?
When people look up to you, as a role model. Be humble.

Any thoughts of a career after football?
Coaching I think, but that's a few years away just yet.

Favourite PS4 or Xbox game?
Fifa.

MASSADIO HAIDARA

Boyhood hero?
Ronaldinho.

Best footballing moment?
Making my debut for Nancy (my first club).

Toughest opponent?
Sergio Aguero.

Team supported as a boy?
Monaco.

Pre-match meal/Favourite food?
Hot chocolate/Chicken and pasta.

Any superstitions?
I pray to God.

Favourite current player?
Lionel Messi.

Favourite other sports person?
Roger Federer.

Favourite stadium other than St. James' Park?
Old Trafford.

What would you be if you weren't a footballer?
Definitely playing another sport.

Where did you go for your 2016 summer holiday?
Dubai and Miami.

What do you like in particular about the city of Newcastle?
I love the city centre, it's a very vibrant city.

Favourite actor/actress?
Leonardo DiCaprio/Blake Lively.

Favourite TV show?
Plus Belle La Vie (French soap opera).

Favourite music artist and last concert seen?
Chris Brown/Nicki Minaj.

What do you like doing in your spare time?
Resting and playing on my Play Station.

Best friend in football?
Ibrahim Amadou (Lille)

Which three people would you invite round for Dinner?
Lionel Messi, Blake Lively and Neymar.

What's the best thing about being a footballer?
Being able to do what you like the best.

Any thoughts of a career after football?
I don't know yet!

Favourite PS4 or Xbox game?
Fifa – it's the best.

MATT RITCHIE

Boyhood hero?
Steven Gerrard.

Best footballing moment?
Getting promoted in 2015 with Bournemouth.

Toughest opponent?
Patrice Evra.

Team supported as a boy?
Portsmouth.

Pre-match meal/Favourite food?
Sweet potato & chicken/Steak.

Any superstitions?
None.

Favourite current player?
Lionel Messi.

Favourite other sports person?
Jason Day.

Favourite stadium other than St. James' Park?
Stamford Bridge.

What would you be if you weren't a footballer?
A golfer.

Where did you go for your 2016 summer holiday?
Tuscany.

What do you like in particular about the city of Newcastle?
The passion of the fans.

Favourite actor?
Tom Hardy.

Favourite TV show?
Peaky Blinders.

Favourite music artist and last concert seen?
Travis for both.

What do you like doing in your spare time?
Golf and relaxing with my family.

Best friend in football?
Callum Reynolds (Boreham Wood)

Which three people would you invite round for Dinner?
Alex Ferguson, President Obama and Fran Healy from Travis.

What's the best thing about being a footballer?
Winning matches with your friends.

Any thoughts of a career after football?
Coaching.

Favourite PS4 or Xbox game?
I don't play.

DWIGHT GAYLE

Boyhood hero?
David Beckham.

Best footballing moment?
The 2016 FA Cup Final day experience.

Toughest opponent?
Nemanja Vidic.

Team Supported as a boy?
Manchester United.

Pre-match meal/Favourite food?
Chicken & rice/Thai green curry.

Any superstitions?
None.

Favourite current player?
Ronaldo.

Favourite other sports person?
LeBron James.

Favourite stadium other than St. James' Park?
Old Trafford.

What would you be if you weren't a footballer?
A carpenter.

Where did you go for your 2016 summer holiday?
Portugal and Thailand.

What do you like in particular about the city of Newcastle?
Everyone is football mad!

Favourite Actor?
Adam Sandler.

Favourite TV Show?
Game of Thrones.

Favourite music artist and last concert seen?
Drake for both.

What do you like doing in your spare time?
Relaxing and playing golf.

Best friend in football?
Fraizer Campbell

Which three people would you invite round for Dinner?
Ronaldo, David Beckham and Alex Ferguson.

What's the best thing about being a footballer?
Doing what you love

Any thoughts of a career after football?
A golfer (hopefully).

Favourite PS4 or Xbox game?
Fifa.

a TO z OF UNITED

Asprilla – Tino was a maverick and his hat-trick against Barcelona will remain etched in the memory of Magpie fans forever.

Burton Albion – United will meet the Brewers for the first time in their history this season, leaving just seven current Football League teams the Magpies have never faced competitively.

Captain – There have been a few great ones down the years; Harvey, Anderson, Iley, Roeder, Beardsley and Shearer, but Bob Moncur remains one of the greatest.

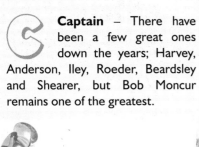

De Jong – The latest set of brothers to have played for United, following in the footsteps of the Ameobi, Appleby, Guthrie, Kennedy, LuaLua, Robledo and Withe brothers. And there are two further sets of brothers in the youth set-up now.

Edgar Street – The venue for possibly the most famous FA Cup upset in the history of the competition in 1972.

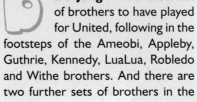

Fifties Glory – United won the FA Cup in 1951, 1952 and 1955, what a great time to be a Magpies fan!

Given – Shay is United's most-capped international player of all time; he won 82 of his 140 Ireland caps whilst at St. James' Park.

Heartbreak – Whether it's relegation, losing the Premier League title or last-minute goals, there's been plenty for the United faithful to suffer down the years.

Inter Milan – United took their largest ever away following to a European game when over 10,000 Geordies travelled to Milan for a Champions League tie in 2003.

Jenas – The 19-year-old made his full Magpies debut in a winning United team at the Stadium of Light in 2002.

King George V – The only reigning monarch to pay a visit to St. James' Park back in 1917.

League Cup Final – United have only appeared in one, 1976, losing 2-1 to Manchester City despite Alan Gowling's goal.

Mirandinha – The first Brazilian player to play in England when he signed for United in 1987.

Newcastle East End – Forerunners of Newcastle United before changing their name to United in 1892.

Quinn – Only three players in United's history with their surname beginning with the letter Q have played for the club, and all were called Quinn; Charles, Mick and Wayne.

Ujpest – United's opponents in the 1969 Fairs Cup Final.

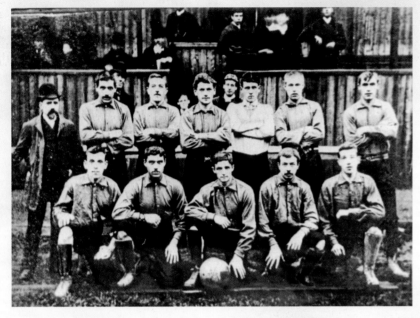

Venison – Barry was a great captain who led United to the Football League Division One title in 1993.

Watson – Steve was United's youngest ever player at 16 years and 223 days when he played against Wolves on 10 November 1990.

Offside – Still causes a huge amount of debate in the game and remember, back in the 1920s, the Football Association had to change the offside law thanks mainly to Bill McCracken's astute play and positioning.

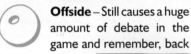

Penalties – The dreaded denouement, United have only won one of their eight competitive penalty shoot-out competitions, against Watford in 2006.

Rafa Benitez – United's Spanish manager.

Shearer – United's all-time leading scorer with 206 goals.

Xisco – The only player in Newcastle's 136-year history to have a surname starting with the letter X.

Yellow – The much-derided changed kit that United wore during their Championship winning season of 2009/10. It didn't serve them that badly, losing only two away games wearing it.

Taylor – Steven and Ryan were both great servants to United in the last decade.

Zola – Not Gianfranco, but Calvin who turned out for United's reserves in 2003/04.

From Academy To First Team

Making the journey from youth to first team football can be an incredibly difficult task. Many don't quite make the grade, but quite often move on to other clubs. For the lucky few – and they are a select band of players who have shown the necessary, skill, dedication, attitude and passion, to name just four of the attributes you need to be a professional footballer – it's a dream come true when they can proudly say 'I played for Newcastle United'.

Here we profile all those players, from the start of the Premier League era in 1992/93 to the present day, in our Academy Montage. Statistics are correct up until August 2016.

Rolando Aarons, 2014-present
17 appearances, 3 goals

Sammy Ameobi, 2011-present
67 appearances, 4 goals

Phil Airey, 2011-2013
1 appearance, 0 goals

Shola Ameobi, 2000-2014
397 appearances, 79 goals

Jak Alnwick, 2014-2015
8 appearances, 0 goals

Matty Appleby, 1990-1994
29 appearances, 0 goals

Adam Armstrong, 2014-present
19 appearances, 0 goals

Andy Carroll, 2006-2011
91 appearances, 33 goals

Paul Dummett, 2013-present
75 appearances, 3 goals

David Beharall, 1999-2002
6 appearances, 0 goals

Michael Chopra, 2002-2006
31 appearances, 3 goals

David Edgar, 2006-2009
23 appearances, 2 goals

Paul Brayson, 1994-1997
2 appearances, 0 goals

Lee Clark, 1988-1997
265 appearances, 28 goals

Robbie Elliott, 1989-1997
188 appearances, 12 goals

Steve Caldwell, 2000-2004
37 appearances, 2 goals

James Coppinger, 2000-2002
1 appearance, 0 goals

Shane Ferguson, 2010-2016
32 appearances, 0 goals

Adam Campbell, 2012-2015
5 appearances, 0 goals

Ryan Donaldson, 2009-2012
6 appearances, 0 goals

Lewis Guy, 2004-2006
1 appearance, 0 goals

Steve Harper, 1993-2013
199 appearances, 0 goals

Tim Krul, 2006-present
185 appearances, 0 goals

Alan Neilson, 1989-1995
50 appearances, 1 goal

Steve Howey, 1986-2000
242 appearances, 7 goals

Kazenga LuaLua, 2008-2012
15 appearances, 0 goals

Alan O'Brien, 2006-2007
9 appearances, 0 goals

Aaron Hughes, 1997-2005
278 appearances, 6 goals

Lomana LuaLua, 2000-2004
88 appearances, 9 goals

Matty Pattison, 2006-2008
15 appearances, 0 goals

Paul Huntington, 2006-2007
16 appearances, 1 goal

Kevin Mbabu, 2015-present
5 appearances, 0 goals

Peter Ramage, 2005-2008
69 appearances, 0 goals

Brian Kerr, 1997-2004
13 appearances, 0 goals

Jamie McClen, 1994-2005
22 appearances, 1 goal

Nile Ranger, 2009-2013
62 appearances, 3 goals

Callum Roberts, 2015-present
1 appearance, 0 goals

James Tavernier, 2009-2014
10 appearances, 0 goals

Steve Watson, 1989-1998
263 appearances, 14 goals

Lubo Satka, 2015-present
1 appearance, 0 goals

Steven Taylor, 2004-2016
268 appearances, 15 goals

NEWCASTLE UNITED

Kevin Scott, 1984-1994
275 appearances, 11 goals

Alan Thompson, 1989-1993
20 appearances, 0 goals

In addition there are a number of players who have come through the Academy, made it into the first-team squad, but didn't (or have yet to) taste first team football.

They are:

Dan Barlaser, Gary Caldwell, Frank Danquah, Mark Doninger, Stuart Elliott, Fraser Forster, Kris Gate, Liam Gibson, Stuart Green, Brad Inman, Peter Keen, Olivier Kemen, Ole Soderberg, Michael Richardson, Remie Streete, James Troisi, Callum Williams and Freddie Woodman.

And of course the likes of Paul Gascoigne, one of United's most famous home-grown players, came through the ranks in the mid-1980s before the introduction of the Premier League.

Jamie Sterry, 2016-present
1 appearance, 0 goals

Haris Vuckic, 2009-present
20 appearances, 1 goal

QUIZ ANSWERS

SPOT THE DIFFERENCE (PAGE 27)

SPOT THE BALL (PAGE 23)

GOING FOR GOAL (PAGE 17)

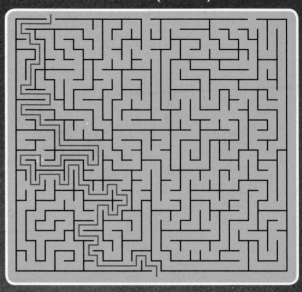

QUIZ ANSWERS (PAGE 21)

Quiz 1
What do you remember about the 2015/16 season?

1. Papiss Cisse
2. Watford
3. Paul Simpson
4. Northampton Town
5. Liverpool
6. 31
7. Mike Williamson
8. Norwich City
9. Jamie Sterry
10. West Ham and Leicester

Quiz 2
See how much you know about Newcastle United's history.

1. Glasgow Rangers
2. Everton
3. Leeds United
4. Rob Lee
5. West Brom
6. Jimmy Lawrence
7. Sunderland
8. Fulham
9. CSKA Sofia
10. Temuri Ketsbaia

WORDSEARCH (PAGE 47)

1 Barnsley
2 Solano
3 Milburn
4 Germany
5 Maracana
6 Robson
7 Beckenbauer
8 Argyle
9 Routledge
10 Argentina
11 Highbury
12 Lovenkrands
13 Strachan
14 Feyenoord
15 Gallacher
16 Uruguay
17 Lampard
18 Rovers
19 Tottenham
20 Linesman

CROSSWORD (PAGE 39)

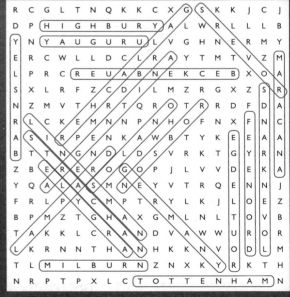